Earth's Changing Coasts

by Neil Morris

Raintree

Chicago, Illinois

Printed and bound in China by South China Printing Company
07 06 05 04 03
10 9 8 7 6 5 4 3 2 1

Editorial: Keith Ulrich
Design: Erica Barraca
Picture Services: Michelle Lisseter and Bridge Creative Ltd
Illustrations: Bridge Creative Services Ltd
Production: Sal D'Amico

Cover photograph of Rio de Janeiro reproduced with permission of Corbis (Wolfgang Kaehler).

The publishers would like to thank
Margaret Mackintosh for her assistance
in the preparation of this book.

Every effort has been made to contact copyright holders of any material reproduced in this book. Any omissions will be rectified in subsequent printings if notice is given to the publishers.

Library of Congress Cataloging-in-Publication Data

Morris, Neil, 1946-
    Earth's changing coasts / Neil Morris.
        p. cm. -- (Landscapes and people)
Summary: Looks at the geography and people that make up coastal regions throughout the world, focusing on the changing characteristics of both. Includes bibliographical references and index.
ISBN 1-4109-0178-5 (hc), 1-4109-0341-9 (pb)
1. Coasts--Juvenile literature. 2. Coast changes--Juvenile literature. 3. Coastal ecology--Juvenile literature. [1. Coasts. 2. Coast changes. 3. Coastal ecology. 4. Ecology. 5. Nature--Effect of human beings on.] I. Title. II. Series: Morris, Neil, 1946-
Landscapes and people.
GB453.M67 2003
910'.914'6--dc21

                            2003006013

Acknowledgments
The publishers would like to thank the following for permission to reproduce photographs:
p. 9, 15 Jeff Foott/Bruce Coleman Collection, p. 20 Judith Clark/Bruce Coleman Collection, p. 27 Pacific Stock/Bruce Coleman Collection; p. 4 Neil Rabinowitz/Corbis, p. 7 Paul A. Souders/Corbis, p. 8 Chris North/Cordaiy Picture Library/Corbis, p. 10 Andrew Brown/Ecoscene/Corbis, p. 14 Gallo Images/Corbis, p. 19 Bettmann/Corbis, p. 26 Anthony Cooper/Corbis; p. 11 Taxi/Toyohiro Yamada/Getty Images, p. 13 Stone/Getty Images, p. 21 Imagebank/Getty Images, p. 22 Taxi/Getty Images, p. 28 Imagebank/Getty Images; p. 29 National Oceanic and Atmospheric Administration; p. 16 John Shaw/NHPA, p. 17 Alan Williams/NHPA, p. 24 Daniel Heuclin/NHPA; p. 6 Martyn Chillmaid/Oxford Scientific Films.

Contents

Any words appearing in the text in bold, **like this,** are explained in the Glossary.

What Is a Coast?

What do you think of when you think of the coast? Does it have sandy beaches, palm trees, and warm blue seas? Does it have high, rocky **cliffs?** Or perhaps it has a busy **harbor** with fishing boats and sailing yachts? Whichever one you think of, you're right. The coast can be all of these things, and many others, too.

More than two-thirds of Earth's surface is covered by oceans and seas. This means that land makes up less than one-third of the surface of Earth. What we call the coast is the place where the ocean or sea meets the land.

*The line of the coast is rarely straight, as this Caribbean shoreline shows. Beaches and **bays** are usually curved, and their shape is constantly changing.*

Around the world

All of the world's great land masses, called **continents,** are surrounded by oceans and have long coastlines. There are seven continents—Africa, Antarctica, Asia, Europe, North America, South America, and Australia. Around these continents are four large oceans—the Pacific, Atlantic, Indian, and Arctic Oceans.

The world's coasts are constantly changing. Where the powerful force of the sea meets the land, waves pound against the **shore,** and gradually wear away at rocks. The waves break off pieces of rock, grind them up, and eventually lay them down somewhere else as dunes or beaches. This changes the shape of our coasts.

Looking at coasts

In this book we look at many different kinds of coasts. We see how they were formed and how they have changed over the years. We look at the animals and plants that live along the coastline, and the ways in which people living beside coasts use and change them.

This map shows the world's continents and oceans. The Southern Ocean, around the frozen continent of Antarctica, is made up of parts of three other oceans.

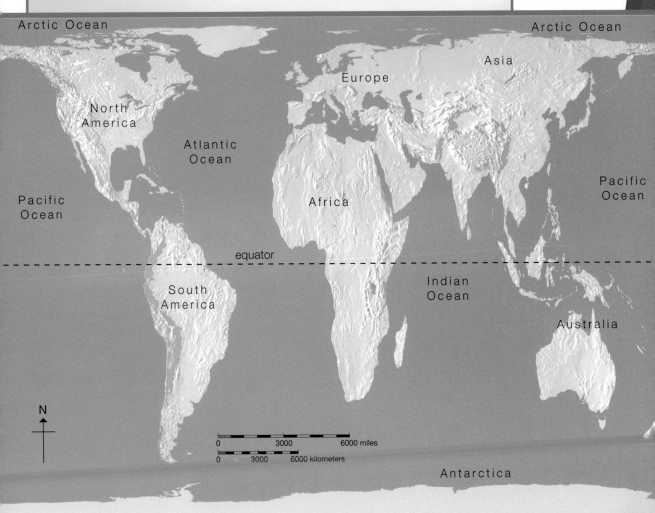

Arctic Ocean

Arctic Ocean

Asia

Europe

North America

Atlantic Ocean

Pacific Ocean

Pacific Ocean

Africa

equator

South America

Indian Ocean

Australia

N

0   3000   6000 miles
0   3000   6000 kilometers

Antarctica

How Do Coasts Form and Change?

The action of the ocean carves the world's coastlines. There are many different kinds of coasts. They vary according to their location in the world. The **climate,** and especially the wind, has a great effect on the ocean. The wind pushes the water into waves and, in turn, the movement of waves affects the coast.

↟ *Over many years the pounding of waves can wear away even the hardest rocks.*

Wave power

Waves are made by wind blowing over the ocean. They may begin as tiny ripples, but by the time they reach the coast, waves can be large and powerful. As a large wave gets close to the **shore,** where the ocean is shallow, its top curves and makes frothy foam called surf. This is a breaking wave, or **breaker.** Breakers move fast and have enormous power. As they hit land, they throw tons of foaming water against the shore.

Wearing away

Water is heavy, so when it moves fast it has great force. This is why waves gradually wear away rocks, in a process called **erosion.** Some rocks are harder than others, and this hardness makes a difference to the effects of erosion. **Cliffs** made of softer rock, such as **chalk,** are worn away more quickly than harder rock, like **granite.** Chalk cliffs crumble away, especially during storms. Water and bubbles are forced into tiny cracks in hard rock cliffs when waves hit them. The waves squash the air into the cracks, like a hammer driving a wedge. This process weakens the rocks and, eventually, pieces break off and fall into the ocean.

As foaming water rushes in and out of cracks in cliffs, day after day, year after year, rocks begin to break up.

Destructive waves

The biggest, most powerful waves are called **tsunamis** (from the Japanese words meaning "**harbor** waves"). A tsunami can move at up to 497 miles (800 kilometers) an hour in the open sea. It can reach heights of more than 98 feet (30 meters) by the time it gets to the shore. Such giant waves are sometimes called tidal waves, but they have nothing to do with tides. They are more often caused by **earthquakes** under the **seabed.** When an earthquake shakes under the sea, it makes waves that race across the ocean. Tsunamis can cause great damage to coasts, throwing rocks onto the shore, washing beaches away, and destroying harbors and houses. Fortunately for people living by the coast, these enormous waves are rare.

Intertidal zones

The intertidal area can be divided into four zones: lower, middle, and upper **shore,** and the splash zone. Each zone has its own kind of life and constantly changes with the tides. The lower shore, near the low tide mark, is covered by water most of the time. Shrimp, snails, and tubeworms live there, as well as many small fish. Further up the slope of the beach, the middle shore is exposed to the air twice a day for a few hours. This is home to **sea anemones,** mussels, and sea urchins. Barnacles, periwinkles, and crabs live on the upper shore. Finally, just above the high-tide mark, is the splash zone. Small winkles and sandhoppers have made this region of sea spray their home.

Tidal pools

Some coasts have a level area of rock at the base of cliffs, called a wave-cut platform (because it is carved out by waves). Very often there are holes in the platform, and water is left there when the tide goes out. We call these holes tidal pools. They are a difficult place for animals to live because of the tide constantly coming in and going out. Nevertheless, some small fish, shrimp, and crabs have **adapted** to this life of constant change. Tidal pools are a good place to observe small wildlife in action, but make sure you watch out for the tide coming in!

Soal

Peop...
prot...
pow...
or b...
tetra...
so th...

Ma

Mo...
fro...
Th...
inc...
on...
alc...
wa...
Na...
fo...

This puffin's beak is full of sand eels it has caught to feed its chicks.

At home by the sea

Many kinds of sea birds make their nests on **cliffs** high above the shore. They crowd together in huge **colonies.** This keeps them safe from much larger birds like the peregrine falcon. Sea birds don't need much space on land because they do all their feeding at sea. Fulmars nest on cliff ledges, and the parents catch most of the fish they need to feed their young by swimming on the surface of the water. Gannets also nest on cliffs, but they fish in a different way—flying down from a great height and diving into the ocean to catch their food.

On top of the cliffs

Puffins also live in large groups. They nest in burrows at the top of cliffs. As with other sea birds, the most important thing about the location of the nest is food. Puffins dive into the ocean to catch small fish underwater.

Index